With These We Will Never Go Hungry

C.L. Flood

With These We Will Never Go Hungry

For my daughters and grandchildren

With These We Will Never Go Hungry
ISBN 978 1 76109 238 1
Copyright © text C.L. Flood 2022
Cover image: *A Bruise for a Bruise*, Eloise Kirk, 2021

First published 2022 by
GINNINDERRA PRESS
PO Box 3461 Port Adelaide 5015
www.ginninderrapress.com.au

Contents

Black Peppermint

I remember the wood. It was peppermint. Black peppermint. Snug inside its bark. Logs, branches and kindling cut from dead trees on the hills enveloping my valley left scattered across my driveway and along the road.

It had been the end of a love affair stunted by the inability to find the words to match the feelings.

He walked away, his long legs striding through an ocean of billowing, uncut grass. His dog nipping relentlessly at his heels and dancing into the back of the ute.

The following day, he wound his way down the road, the dog barking maniacally on top of a wood pile to announce their arrival.

'I won't accept your charity,' I shrieked as I swung through the screen door.

Deafened by emotion, he stood legs astride the wood pile, pushing each log to the ground with the side of his boot.

'Damn you. I don't want your wood,' I cried as I picked up the peppermint, piece by piece, hurling it back onto the rusted tray.

The dog spun with excitement, barking in a constant monotone yelp.

'Just take it. Please.'

'I won't appease your guilt.'

Hot tears ran down my face, my fingers smarting as I threw each log back towards him.

A herd of black and white cattle stood at my fence, watching the wood flying on and off the ute like a game of tennis. Their eyes wide, benign. Their jaws moving from side to side. Clouds of cold air blowing in and out of their velvet nostrils.

My little girl stood at the door crying.

He jumped off the tray, scrambled into the cabin and started the engine without shutting the back flap, and drove away, logs flying off onto the road, shattering behind him. His dog stood steady on what remained of the wood pile, his bark echoing through the valley.

I remember the wood. It was peppermint. Black peppermint. My little girl slept heavily on my arm as we sat sunken into a cushioned wicker chair by the fire. Alone. White wood burned red and hot. Lost words crackled through the flames.

The Emancipation of René

We set up house in an old timber mill in the New England ranges, splinting and bandaging our relationship with an ideal.

Vic painted 'green' political banners in a studio decorated with sacks of rescued orphaned eastern grey joeys. We shouted at each other in competition with the sulphur-crested cockatoo, crippled by a log truck. An echidna had made its home beneath our woodpile, rendering it useless and us cold. A wombat joey crept into our bed, spreading an invisible mite as her revenge for the loss of her mother. We bathed in a foul solution, scratched at our microscopic invader and boasted to our friends of our bucolic lifestyle.

René came to us from a bankrupt wildlife park, gnashing his canine teeth and emitting an acrid smell, apparently attractive to vixens.

Vic built him a run beneath the kitchen window, which was either a mistake or a taunt.

'It's a beautiful smell. We should bottle and sell it – the ultimate aphrodisiac,' he declared, challenging me with his ice-blue eyes. There was fury in his gaze and tone I hadn't seen at the beginning but it wasn't new.

'Poor René, caged and frightened,' I thought out loud.

'Jesus Christ, girl, an introduced species for some fools to play the hunt. He eliminates our native species and causes havoc in the environment.'

There was no homecoming for the fox. René wasn't responsible for man's sporting folly and yet faced culling. I made a mistake and faced gossip and brief social shunning.

I squatted down beside his pen and his head popped out from the hollow log which was now his den. A fox can hear a mouse squeak up to thirty metres away and it seemed René could hear my thoughts. His gaze met mine and, as if we'd met our doppelganger, our thoughts transposed.

Long ago, when he was free, they had come from the grey-brown scrub, hooves lifting above the toppled dead gums, thundering on in pursuit, onto the endless grass plain. The vixen crouched beneath a pile of rocks and he ran, swiftly, skilfully placing his back paws into front paw tracks, doubling back to confuse and escape the hounds and the dry-mouthed, mounted men.

In his territory, he and the vixen played throughout the winter in the long grass celebrating their escape. Seven pups were born in the early spring and together they had hunted and fed on carrion and rodents. They stalked live prey by the slender light shafts of the moon bringing home live field mice for the pups to play with in preparation for hunting. They drank from the rivulets and dams and travelled for miles with the breeze against their faces. Free.

A short bark broke the spell.

René paced for days, snarling at Vic but eating from my hand. I stroked his coat and touched his underfur, soft as the down on the nape of a baby's neck. He had attempted an escape though a thin slit in the pen's slats, leaving tufts of red hair as a reminder of his breakout's futility.

As my affection for René grew, so did Vic's agitation.

'You climb in, clean out his pen. Let's see how brave you really are.' He'd begun demanding displays of courage in return for his diminishing affection.

René danced to the back of the pen, folding his front paws in amusement as I moved the door's rusting hinges. I crawled in on all fours and washed his concrete floor. Every day, he'd picked up his plastic water container in his teeth and spilled it. I crawled out, filled it once more leaving the door open, just wide enough for the captive, not the captor, to see.

I went inside and watched the brown dam water wash the dirt from my hands. I picked up my handbag and threw it around my shoulder and walked out the back door, past the empty fox pen to the car.

I whispered a goodbye which was tossed up into the tall gums, swaying in the wind like great drunken giants.

I started the engine and drove away.

Darling Lily

A dun foal is born in the night in a stable lit by a near full moon. Quaking with shock, she struggles onto her legs and finds a splayed, tenuous balance. Its mother licks away the afterbirth and pushes her to her teat.

We watch from a distance. Light drizzle sifts from the sky and settles on our coats until they gleam like the newly licked filly. Shivering, we watch the mare and her foal and our eyes moisten. The back of his hand brushes mine and I relish in the little warmth emanating from this cold man's touch. How lonely, a loveless life.

Perched top of the arena rail, I watched the sheep judging. A roughrider shuffled towards me, nudging me softly with his elbow whispering something about a patch of wildflowers behind the stables.

'Darling Lilies.'

I shrugged my shoulders, my eyes fixed on the parade. Young men led their rams around the ring. Some of them were no more than ten years old and they strutted and swaggered like grown men.

'Your name must be Lily? Lily Darling?'

'No, it's Bella.'

'Darling Bella Lily. A bed of Darling Bella Lilies.'

Like a fool, I turned and engaged. He said he saw me jump and liked what he saw, strange as my horse clipped the wall and refused the double.

'You have a good seat.'

'Flattery is the lime to catch a human fly,' my father's voice echoed inside my head.

'Spidery flowers stand up like fence posts. The flower, the stalk, the petal are just decorations like a pretty girl sitting up straight and tall on the rails.'

I smiled.

'Your white blouse, the petals. Your jodhpurs, the stalk. Your boots the earth,'

I laughed.

'But Darling Bella Lily, it's the inside that interests me. The filament, the anther, and the style. That's where life is, inside.'

'You some kind of a poet?'

If I didn't know better, I'd have thought he was talking about the unsettling warmth in my belly and I blushed. He urged me to follow and I did.

'A song of love is a sad song,' he sang.

'Not a bad voice for a roughrider. So where are these flowers? The lilies?'

'Right here,' he said, handing me a silver flask. 'Take a swig.'

I'd never tasted liquor in my life and shook my head.

'Go on, try it.'

It stung my tongue.

'Take another, go on. A big swig.'

I swallowed and my blood burned.

'Hi-lili, high-lili, hi-lo.'

His voice ran over me like treacle and he draped his arm around me, pulled my face to his and kissed me deeply. His tongue tasted of liquor as it roamed around my mouth and I pulled away. He reeled me in again then ran his hands over my body and I gasped and uttered a muffled plea to stop but he didn't. I heard the sound of the hurdy-gurdy in the distance, the clink-clank of the rides, his moaning in my ear.

We leave mother and foal to come and go as they please for the next six months, content in each other's company.

From time to time, I venture close, staying low to the ground. Staying against her mother's flank the foal moves in and sniffs my hand tentatively. At first, she throws her head up and squeals but soon lets me stroke her forelock and neck in exchange for a nibble of whatever's in my hand.

He said a wife would come in handy on the place.

'Your mother would be turning in her grave you taking up with a bloke like that but you've made your bed,' Dad said, shaking his head, as he hands me over to the gimlet-eyed cowboy.

He begins handling and sacking out the foal while I sand and paint her stable. My work is shoddy and my brushstrokes irresolute, he says, picking at every bump not sanded, every crack unfilled. I've learned silence lest he deliver the pointy end of his tongue or the back of his hand.

He runs his rough hands over the length and breadth of the foal's body, just as he does mine. He spends his nights gobbling at me like a starved hog, pushing his face into my neck, panting in my ear. I learn to rise above it, moving like an automaton, my eyes fixed on the ceiling, studying my bewilderment.

As the stable takes on colour, the atmosphere darkens. Winter shakes the leaves from the trees and I wear bruises beneath my great-coat.

He drags, pushes, stops her then changes direction, taping her hooves and lifting her legs to desensitise her. He halters her with a rope secured around her rump. She cries out, pig rooting, stamping and foaming until finally, he wears her down and wide-eyed, she submits. He hobbles her, tying ropes around her legs, fixing her to the rails. She snorts at the sight of the bridle. He runs it over her face before forcing a homemade twitch over her swollen muzzle. The foal is frozen in pain. He pushes the bit between her teeth and the crown over her ears. He tightens the chinstrap and loosens the twitch. Then he drops a saddle on her too-young back.

'It's too soon. She's not yet one,' I tell him but he knows horses, he says, tightening the girth.

'This is when you break them,' he announces.

He loosens the ropes and she rears and gathers herself in panic and takes the fence coming down hard on the rail, opening her fetlock. She stumbles back onto her feet and gallops across the paddock. We make chase but there's no catching her.

'She'll come back when she's hungry. She knows where to get a good feed,' he says.

I spend the night tuned to every breaking stick, every whinny.

After three long nights, the filly limps through the morning frost to the stables. I go to her and stroke her nose and ease off the bridle then loosen the girth and slide the saddle from her abraded back. I run my hand down her neck, shoulder and over her leg and she lifts it and I hold her fetlock in my hands. I clean the blood from the wound and whisper in her ear while she nudges me gently. I take a tin of Stockholm tar from the shelf and coat the open flesh.

'You think you're a horseman?' he barks, knocking the tin out of my hands with one swipe. He storms away shouting expletives and I pick up the tin and tend to the filly daily until she heals.

'That leg's looking good. Time for your ride,' he says.

'Oh no, she's not broken in.'

'Neither are you. Now kit up.'

I do as I'm told.

Fastening my jodhpurs around my ever decreasing waist with a belt, I pull on my dress boots and button up a clean blouse.

'Priceless,' he laughs, banging a helmet so hard onto my head that my ears ring.

The filly dances backwards and he raises a welt on her withers and throws the saddle over her back and tightens the girth. She passes wind.

I extend my hand towards her and she hangs her head. I move around her and we smell each other's fear.

'Alley-up.' He hoists me into the saddle.

I feel her shudder from her tail, along her back to her neck and watch her mane quiver and I feel her ready for flight.

He opens the gate. 'Take her around the paddock, National Velvet.'

Holding the reins softly so as not to hurt her mouth, I rock in the saddle to move her on and she jumps into a trot. I rise and stand in the stirrups so as not to damage her back. I round the yard and her trot steadies and I loosen the reins.

'I said the paddock!'

I round the yard again.

He strides towards us, dust flying about him. He kicks her in the belly and she rears. I slide over the cantle, hit the ground and he lets out a high-pitched feverish cackle, slapping his thighs.

'Did they teach you that at Pony Club?'

The filly freezes, flashing the whites of her eyes. He grabs the reins and jerks the bit again and again until her mouth foams blood. I catch her pleading eye. I struggle to my feet and shove him in the back. He stands still for a moment then swings around and swats me like a fly. Staggering back onto my feet, I peel off my helmet and throw it at him but it misses and skips across the yard. I run into the house and pick up the telephone, not knowing who to call. I hear the filly's cries and the dial tone whines in my ear.

'Oh God,' I wail. 'Who can I call? I don't know who to call.'

I dial the number I know by heart.

I wait and watch a pall of dust rise along the road.

Krapoot Lek

I was in love with love. Donning lycra, gloves and a helmet, I fixed my feet to the pedals in cleats and trained in the hill country. I packed and boarded a flight to Chiang Mai and a bus to Mae Sai on the Burmese border.

We cycled south through the Golden Triangle alongside the Mekong River in searing heat, rendering my lycra useless and my skin blotched, raised and itchy. I bought a cotton shirt and discarded my helmet for a peaked cap and wrapped my burning neck in a scarf soaked in water.

Villagers along the way regarded me with suspicion. The Buddhist chanting from the village wats sounded a contradiction. A Western woman, I soon learned, was an oddity.

He rode beside me sharing his love of cycling. 'I couldn't be with someone who didn't love cycle touring,' he said, throwing down the gauntlet.

As my skin and confidence peeled, he distanced himself plugging into Thai lessons on his iPod.

'This,' he declared over a bowl of chilli entrails, 'is our new home.'

The large brown bird landed beside me and spread its bright chestnut wings. Its body was black, glossed with purple and its eyes ruby red. It pecked at some fallen fruit until it was sated then boomed, 'Coop-coop-coop.'

'What bird is that?' I asked.

'Krapoot lek,' he replied.

'Oh,' too timid to repeat the words.

'A cuckoo. If you hear it in the morning, it's good luck.'

'And in the afternoon?'

The bird boomed again. 'Coop-coop-coop.' From that point on, krapoot leks were everywhere.

We were staying. We would rent a house in Chiang Mai and retire. We could live cheaply with servants to cook and clean and we could do as we pleased. No chores. No responsibilities.

I cycled through the loneliest and longest month of my life with an eager smile fixed to my face.

He quickly picked up the tongue and began conversing with the locals who buzzed around him like the mosquitoes around our bed.

The women giggled, 'Kop kun ka,' bowing their heads, their long black glossy hair toppling over their hands pressed in prayer position.

'Coop, coop, coop.'

I watched the cuckoo forage for insects and fallen fruit as I foraged for something to say.

The rainy season arrived early and I sweated beneath a plastic poncho for the good part of a week. We had planned our first night back in Chiang Mai in a hotel with Australian network television and a Western bathroom.

With one more mountain to climb, we cycled along an undulating road amid jujube farms. It was harvest time. The women called out to him and waved, their laughter rising as we cycled towards its base.

'What are they saying?' I asked but he didn't reply.

The bitumen stopped at the base and we dismounted, faced with seven kilometres of mud to push our bikes through. I wanted to turn back and take an alternate route. He didn't.

'One more hill to go. This is what touring is all about,' he said. We were out of water, having either drunk it or poured it over our sizzling skin. We pushed without stopping, as there were swarms of mosquitos waiting for a stationary pink-fleshed landing strip. I cried out to God for help and found Him both as silent and uncooperative as my partner.

At the peak, we hung our heads over our handlebars, catching our breath. We noticed the bitumen resumed on a perilously steep decline into the sprawling city below.

'Now for the fun part, I'll show you how to ride down,' he said.

'It's too steep. I'm walking,' I answered.

'Aren't you even going to try?' he snapped, mounting with a wide swing of his muscular, mud-splattered leg and rode brakeless and careless down the hill.

'Coop-coop-coop,' the bird boomed beside me with a mouthful of jujube. It seemed to be saying, 'I couldn't be with someone who didn't love cycle touring,'

'I hate it!' I cried, hiding my face in my hands.

'Coop-coop-coop.'

Carrying the weight of failure, I walked the bike down the hill to the plain below and cycled into to Chiang Mai alone. With the help of English-speaking tourists, I found our hotel. He had checked in and left the spare key at reception. The room was empty but I saw that he had showered, his wet towel draped across the bed. The contents of his panniers lay strewn across the floor. I left mine packed, save a pair of pants, clean cotton shirt and a pair of sandals. I showered, dressed and walked the streets until I found a travel agent and booked the first flight home.

Follow the Shadows

A workaholic, I was showing signs of burnout. I was told to take a holiday.

'There's too much work,' I argued, but my business partner told me a colleague would cover my role.

'There's nothing else I want to do,' I said, and she suggested I spend a week helping her son in the outback.

'Sam needs an organiser. Someone like you to start his engine,' she said.

The conversation was over.

I had met Sam several times before when he'd come to town to renegotiate the terms of his mortgage. He was struggling in the drought.

Leaving the city behind, I drove ten hours north-west into flat, stricken land. It was wheat country, or so it had been when the fields of grain danced in the rain. A time when harvests didn't fail. Now it was parched split earth.

I turned at the homestead's sign and drove over a corrugated dirt road to a dilapidated weatherboard house. Sam welcomed me with an awkward hello. He was as I remembered him. Big and shy. Only now he was unshaven. Despondency etched on his face. In a clumsy show of hospitality, he made me a plate of sandwiches and a cup of tea. He showed me to my room at the far end of the house.

Sleep saw dreams of white lines and blurred landscape and I woke to a hot sunrise streaming through the window. The sky bright blue. Not a cloud. No memory of rain.

I got up and walked through the house to find Sam sunken into an armchair, his demeanour drooping like the bull-nose veranda around his house. His broad brow flecked with sunspots and his hands scored.

'Make yourself at home,' he murmured, resigned to my presence.

I threw back a coffee and began by running a damp cloth over every piece of furniture in the house, sinking the dust into a bucket of hot water. I swept and mopped the floors, vacuumed the carpets, scrubbed off the bath scum and scoured algae from the toilet bowl. The house creaked and groaned, uncomfortable with its bustling intruder. Sam watched the dust settle back onto the surfaces I had just cleaned.

The kitchen was a health hazard hungry for repair. The walls and shelves tacky with creosote and fat; the stove black with grime. I skipped breakfast and took the ute into the sleep town, some fifty kilometres west, and bought a bag of sugar soap, a scraper, two brushes and a drum of white paint. The slow, blowsy shopkeeper looked from me to Sam's ute parked outside and back and the corners of her mouth twisted into a smirk.

Back at the house, I was soon in a sweat as I scrubbed and scraped back the walls. My face turned puce. Sam watched my frenzy from his chair, his face blank, impervious. I saw him turn to the window and look at the land outside, shimmering in the searing heat.

A gleam flickered in his eyes and then he rose, went outside, slamming the screen door behind him. He came back with a ladder. He unpacked the cupboards and cleared the shelves. Together we painted the kitchen. We lined the cupboards with newspaper and repacked them.

'I'm buggered and there's drenching to be done,' he sighed.

Through the window I could see a distant mob of dusty backed sheep grazing on saltbush.

'I'll do the mustering,' I offered, and Sam looked back at me smiling.

'Ride a quad bike?' he asked, and I nodded, lying.

'The dog'll help.'

Unchaining a scrawny kelpie from its kennel, he started the bike and pointed me in the direction of the back gate. 'Go west, follow the fence line, through three gates and bring in the mob. I'll meet you at the sheds.'

It was flat country. No landmarks.

'Where are the sheds? How will I find them?'

'By then, the sun will be setting. Follow the shadows.'

The dog barked wildly and jumped onto the bike's tray. It panted and poked me with its cracked-leather nose as I kangaroo-hopped the bike over grids and corrugations.

Carcasses lined the track. Sheep, rabbits and roos. A lone crow flew listlessly above, its belly full of carrion. I sang as I drove through that cemetery. Song allayed my fears and I sang until I was hoarse.

I saw a sudden beauty in the desolation and I stopped, turned off the engine and listened to the bleak country's sounds. Goannas' tails slapping the dirt. The beat of crows' wings. The feeble spring of starved roos.

Dismounting, I lay on my back and covered my face with Sam's hat. I smelled his sweat. The scent of his labour, of the land. The scent of the years. I felt my racing city pulse slow, marking time with the ancient earth.

The sun moved across the sky, elongating the shadows. Pointing. I sat up, flipped off the lid of my water bottle and drank. Pouring the last drops over my hat, it fell like rain through the straw and I found myself laughing. Joyous.

Bleating rang through the air and I stood and whistled for the dog. I started the bike and whistled again and it looked at me mockingly before it turned and ran back the way we'd come. Leaping roly-polies, scurrying underneath fences.

'Traitor!' I yelled.

I drove on and found the mob sheltering beneath a grove of gum trees. I pushed them along the dappled line of shadows until the shearing sheds appeared on the horizon like a mirage.

Sam stood in the shade, his dog beside him, a drench gun slung over his shoulder. He whistled and the dog woke and began work, circling, stalking, pushing the sheep through the gate.

'Not bad,' he said. ''Bout three-quarters of 'em.'

It was then I realised that I was not there to help but to receive it.

The Green Room

The old man drifts away like a sea mist. In his mind, he runs his hand over his long board, stroking it as he would the curve of his wife's back.

He surfed every day. It was his ritual, his meditation.

He remembers the big sets ruffling the horizon, surfing until he dropped. He sees his younger self at the water's edge, waxing his board, one eye on the break. The wax soft and pliant. Rubbing sand across the board to roughen the surface for grip.

He knows she is watching him. The honey-skinned girl. Her round face, the gleam in her eyes when he tells her the break's a left-hander. Perfect for a goofy like him.

Her laugh.

'A what?'

'Watch.'

Lying flat on the sand, then springing into a crouch, arms outstretched. 'Right foot forward – a goofy. Set for the barrel.'

Her expression, caught between charmed and amused.

He plunges into the icy southern water. Gasping as it floods his wetsuit then slowly warms against his body. Wading out until the foam pounds his chest, then heaving himself onto the board and shifting his weight to plane. Padding out in the rip and crossing over to the break he strokes into a solid eight-footer. The powerful grip. The drop. A bottom turn and back up the wall.

There are people around the bed. Tiptoeing in and out of the room. Touching his hand. Murmuring. But all he hears is the roar and hiss of the foam tumbling behind him as he lets the board stall. The wave curls above him and he tucks into the barrel.

His breathing slows. She sits beside him, stroking his sun-spotted skin, thin as tissue paper. Hers now as freckled as his, that honey-skinned girl knee-deep in the frigid sea, hair loose, knotted by the wind. She waves as he shifts to the front of the board and disappears into the green room.

The Bus Shelter

Every morning, I see her sitting in the bus shelter in town. Head hung over her knees, staring at the ground. Huddled under a pallid winter morning. The sepia light foreshadowing a bleak day.

Pausing, I wonder if she is drunk or high. I consider giving her money but think she'd only drink or smoke it and I move on.

Usually, I enjoy my morning walk. Seeing familiar faces greet one another on the street with a nod and a hello. Hearing clichés about the weather. Knowing my longing to leave this town is foiled by a bothersome bond. This place is in my blood.

Today I'm tempted by the aroma of coffee. I push open the heavy doors of my favourite café, smile at the waiter and sit. He saunters to my table, stands and cocks his head.

'A long black and a biscuit please,' I say and indifference buckles his brow.

He returns with a steaming cup and a small almond biscuit, dusted with icing sugar, which I soak in my coffee, push hurriedly into my mouth and relish the warmth of the coffee's rising steam.

My stomach turns as I think of her, wondering when she last ate or had a hot drink.

Rumour has it Sydney moved its homeless west for the Olympic Games, removed the stain out west so as not to spoil the view. Bussed the lot of them out there to the back of Bourke, into near ghost towns surrounded by arid country as flat as a strap.

Finishing my coffee, I pay at the counter and leave the shop and hurry on.

She remains huddled, expressionless in the bus shelter.

I reach inside my purse and hold out a ten-dollar note. 'Here,' I say, 'take it.'

She doesn't respond.

'Take it please.'

'What for?' Her voice is like mine. Educated, middle-class. Her breath is foul. There are patches of scum on her teeth. Scabs have formed on her skin, exposed to the cold by threadbare clothing.

'Please,' I repeat.

'Piss off.'

I drop the note on the ground beside her, turn and hurry away, confused and humiliated. I vow never to give her money again. I will look the other way as I pass. I will blind myself to her with my belly full and my body warmly clad while she shivers in the frigid winter sun.

The Face

She sat perched on the arm of a worn, green velvet sofa watching. Her father at the controls of a slide projector propped up on a leather-bound book. Once she was a child, she knew this because she saw herself as an image projected onto the irregular surface of a white, stucco wall. The room was dark except for the illuminated image. The dust of aged memories tumbled in a shaft of light.

Familiar voices laughed and muttered stories of the images before them. A family gathered in the shadow of denial and contradiction. The smell of time burned hot.

There on the wall was the child. Pale, tall, her legs splayed to either side of an old wooden dinghy. Green checked shorts, damp and creased, pulled tight against her thighs. A stained white T-shirt billowed about her like the sails on her father's yacht. A rope, taut, strong and twisted, held the dinghy to the yacht. An umbilical cord not yet severed. Tawny hair, matted as salt strap weed on the beach, blew back from a head thrown back in petulant innocence. Eyes dark and unquestioning, squinted towards the sun. Long skinny fingers touched the cool green water. She was that child. She heard them say her name.

'What a waif she was.'

'What a grub she is.'

'A pirate. Ahoy there, me hearty.'

They laughed. She toppled and somersaulted across the carpet. She found her balance again, stood and looked deep into the image on the wall listening for its sounds, its story. She felt its pain.

The ropes and cables tinkled against the aluminium mast, the canvas smacked the wind like sheets on a clothes line. The ocean split behind the dinghy, rolling together with the rise and fall of the waves as though its flesh had split and healed without scarring. The ocean's liquid zipper.

Translucent creatures floated in the current. Blue, white and purple; tentacles reaching out and retracting with the swell. Their sting never quite reaching, never touching. Their might unknown.

The water's spray cooled her back against a sinister memory.

She liked to sail with her father, her face to the wind. Her mother was afraid. She knew better. She was brave. She found approval and admiration in her daring.

'Always was.'

Her father, he is two people, she knew this, she remembered.

Saltwater pushed against her nose, slipping in and out of her nostrils with each quickening breath. Creeping in, slipping down the back of her throat.

'What are you doing, Daddy? Stop!'

The staccato beating of a crumpled child, bent over the deck by a man who once held her in his arms and stroked the tiny hairs on the nape of her neck. Tears of rapture in his eyes. Now he hits her with a strip of the rigging. The yacht rocks hard. They are alone against an expanse of water. The marina gone, land a speck in the distance. Her mother gone.

'Mummy!'

His skin, pungent with the malaise of his pleasure, rubs its stench onto her. He pulls at her shorts and pushes her knees into the ridges of the deck. The pain is sharp, penetrating her artlessness. The pain is wretched. The weight intolerable.

Her nostrils close to the air, foul and thick with his transgression. His chest expands and heaves and his little girl turns to see beads of sweat sitting quaintly on his lip. His neck flushes with shame.

'I will make you brave, not like your mother. I'll show you, you'll never forget. Now, get below and clean yourself up. Get below. Now.'

His voice is low and hoarse, shouting as though she had committed the crime. She remembers and still fails to comprehend. She is bruised and inexplicably wet. There is blood, on her knuckles, on her knees, in her shorts.

The slide on the wall sits too long inside the projector as they remember. She stares in silence. Her father's finger frozen to the projector button, he cannot change the slide. He cannot change what was. He moans deep within his chest.

A slide burns brown and the image on the wall curls and disappears into a stark white light, white stucco wall.

The rope snaps and the cord is severed and the dinghy jerks, tips and turns.

She squeezes her eyes tigh and a little girl dives into the blue water, wrapping herself in the ocean through the face of a wave.

'Get below. Get below.'

Cool water covers the hairs on her body and bubbles form and pull each one out, floating them to the surface. Obtuse faced fish watch and dart and gobble. Her soft skin thickens and turns brown. Speckled and exotic. She sinks to the sandy bottom and lays like a skate, flat and safe.

A groper purses its fleshy lips and slopes off into the murky outskirts. Seahorses vacuum the sand, unperturbed by her presence. Froth moves about her like spores. The yacht distant. Her father's voice mute. Her fingers are webbed, leathery. Her lungs fill with water and float away like jellyfish. Blubbery and flaccid. Tiny gills open and close behind cartilage at the side of her head where once were ears. Warm currents move and caress her.

She is fish, mother ocean cradles her in her voluminous arms and rocks her to sleep.

Old Skin

The air rose hot, thick with pollen and wild with a cacophony of insect song. Green hills lay languid under a hot breeze, their grasses moving like waves.

I sat with my legs tucked into my chest, resting my chin in the neat hollow on the top of my knees as I had done as a child, cooling my feet in a shaded rocky pool. My toes wrinkling and whitening.

Upstream, the river was heavy with the weight of cattle, livid with the heat. Their hooves clattered as they clambered across the river stones in search of the shade of willows. Wattlebirds squawked among the engulfing blackberries, gorging on the fruit, dropping red-stained, seeded excrement back onto the earth. The glorious song of a grey butcherbird rang through the valley.

I watched leaves float along the pool like small boats. Their crisp corners curled towards the sun.

I had just left the dead body of my mother. Her chest stilled. She was gone and I was numb with shame at my fear of abandonment.

A bead of sweat trickled down my forehead and down my cheek and fell into the pool, disturbing a dragonfly poised just above the water's surface. It flew towards me and hovered before my face, examining me through multifaceted eyes. I moved to brush it away then hesitated, held still by the wonder of its close proximity. Each set of its wings moved independently and flickered an iridescent network of tiny green veins. I held my breath so as not to frighten it and at that moment I became what I saw.

Crawling through the mud and mire on the bottom of the pool; as a tiny egg grown into a fat nymph, I shed my skin. I sat and ate, propelling myself with jets of water though tiny gills at the end of my abdomen. I watched for prey creeping along the murky bottom until I was close enough to unhinge my clever lip, grasp it in mouth and devour it.

No thoughts, no emotions, no memory of my mother's cashmere-shrouded breast pressed against my cheek. Her large rough hands linked together at my back holding me. Her ear against mine as though listening for the ocean in a seashell.

Months passed when an ancient restlessness called me in the night. I crawled from the pool to a rock and perched. My outer skin cracked and split and my adult body squeezed from the crusted form that was myself. Born again through the smallest canal, I clung to my shell, breathing air through a row of little holes along my abdomen. Blood began to pump from within my body to fill my veins and my wings dried and stiffened.

A cancer had found its way into my mother, devouring her from the inside out. Now she was laid out. Nurses listened for a silent heart, snipped stitches and pulled out tubes, pinching her flesh like cruel children. I took her clothes to my face and smelled her one last time. I left her, drove home and walked to the river.

We had said goodbye. I had kissed her face and watched a long breath become her last. I had come to the river, my temple, for solace.

The sun touched my wings and their myriad colours glistened at the day. I stretched and flew. My body long and weightless, my flight skilled. The metamorphosis complete.

A heavy sigh fell from my mouth; I heaved and filled my lungs. Alone. Motherless.

I reached down and held my feet and rocked myself back and then just far enough forward to see the reflection of a woman, resembling another just past, grown into her old skin.

Brown Trout

They hiked across the mountains to the Snowy River. Scrambling over rocks and traversing narrow tracks for miles. There were years when the snow fell early and they crossed wide drifts and frozen creeks. Father and daughter. Fishing rods resting on their shoulders. Khakis. Walking boots. Matching Tyrolean hats, decorated with dry flies.

He had never said he wanted a son but as she was the last in a line of daughters, he taught her things he might have done a boy. Fly-fishing was one.

At the river, they balanced on rocks, as far from the bank as they could, moving upstream with stealth. He taught her to cast into the current edges or into a pool near a large rock. She practised casting until she could drop her fly within inches of a protective rock so the fly floated along the current with a perfect drift. There she learned to wait, wholly focused for the take to jerk up the rod tip and set the hook.

This Easter brought with it a chilly wind from the south, mist wisps threatening change. An impending white-out.

He checked his map for the nearest emergency hut. 'We should get to Seaman's,' he said.

'Shh. I can see her.' The fish's brassy brown-spotted body turning, flashing just beneath the surface.

'It's sleeting,' he said and watched her lean back, lift the rod and hook the trout.

'Four pounds at least,' she grinned with a sparkling mouthful of braces.

'Won't be many more trips like this,' he said.

'Why?'

'The dam,' he said, but the real reason was he could see the woman emerging from his little girl. He knew it would not be long before she would fly the nest and he would fish alone.

'That dam. Snowy won't flow for much longer.' He unhooked the fish and wrapped it in plastic and tucked it inside his pack. 'Rug up and let's get back onto the track before it closes in.'

They both knew the danger. In a white-out, they could easily lose their way.

Skin smarting from the sleet and icy wind, they hiked the track high on the Etheridge Range until they came to the little rock hut. It had been built by a man who had lost his son in the 1920s and had sheltered many climbers, skiers and fishermen.

She lit the fire inside and warmed her freezing fingers against the climbing flames while he gutted the fish on a rock outside the hut.

'Get some butter in the pan,' he called as he came inside, cradling the fish in his hands.

They squatted by the fire and watching the fish sizzle in the frypan. When it was cooked, she scooped it onto tin plates and they ate.

'That's one fine catch,' he said. 'One fine catch.'

Home

'I want to go home. Home, I want to go home,' the old man wailed from the confines of his wheelchair. He had been a marathon runner. Now his knees were locked tight with swollen muscles and twisted cartilage.

Beads of sweat covered his face, running down his neck and sagging chest, seeping into his towelling dressing gown. 'I want to go home. Home, I want to go home,' he cried as a nurse wheeled him into the sunroom, closing the door behind him to muffle his cries. 'Home, I want to go home.'

I drove southward, over a range of green hills dotted with apple orchards and black and white cattle and wound my way down into a small town in the Huon Valley. Its main street as wide as the eyes gawking at the sight of a stranger. Beside the narrow, winding road, a grey-green river. Willows hung over its banks, their roots sucking the rippling liquid and shading a herd of cattle. The soil's boggy perfume permeated the air.

'Eyes on the road.' I heard the memory of my father's voice, as stern as caution from his pursed lips. Muscles twitching along his jawline. I looked at the white lines. 'Keep to the left. Keep to the left,' he chanted, jangling the coins in his pocket nervously.

I pulled over in front of a deserted farmhouse gate. A white goshawk watched me from a eucalypt bough. As I climbed the locked gate, it started, spreading its ghostly wings before taking flight. Over and away. I walked through the long grass towards the house and turned to watch the surface of river ripple at the wind's command.

'I could live out here,' I thought out loud.

I peeked through the tear of a lace curtain into an empty room. I walked around the house looking through each window. I tried a door at the back of the house and found it unlocked. Moving quietly through each room, I smelled the dust and grime of an age ago. The kitchen was high-ceilinged, its walls yellowed. A cabinet held a cluster of silver trophies, toppled and tarnished, barely visible through the dusted glass. A stack of newspapers sat in the corner reaching up towards the Baltic pine ceiling strung with cobwebs like mistletoe. I picked up a silk purse I found on the windowsill.

'You right there?' someone called.

I turned to see a wrinkled face, worn from the sun, ruddy.

'Oh, the door was open. I'm sorry. Is this your place?'

'No worries, love. This was my neighbour's. The old man left it to me in his will. Had no family. He lived here all his life till they carried him off to a nursing home in town. Poor old fella couldn't look after himself. His legs gave way, of course. Marathons. Never married.'

I could still hear him. See him.

'Home. I want to go home. To the Huon.'

'Keep quiet or you'll go back in the sunroom,' the nurse snapped.

I held his hand and whispered in his hoary ear, 'Don't you worry, I won't put you in there.'

My fingers moved across his translucent skin. Most of his body hair had long gone, leaving him smooth, soft and silken.

He looked up at me with watery eyes. 'Take me home.'

I pulled back the chequered cover and rolled his pyjama pants up to his thighs and massaged his calves with warm oil.

'Tell me about your running.'

'A long way. Just kept on running. Gotta keep going. Beginning to end. Or you stop. Just kept on running. A long way. Now I can't, I can't. I want to go home. Take me home.'

I walked the corridors of his home, watching the river moving softly through the torn curtains. The purse in my hand like his skin. I slipped it in my pocket.

'You're home now,' I whispered.

I walked back through the grass, pulled a freesia from its roots and slipped it in my mouth and began to suck. I sat for a moment clutching the purse to my chest and then started the car, turned it back towards the city, towards my home.

Dark Night

Colour fades, the very pulse of existence becomes thready, reason is as distant as love lost.

It was my dark night. I was sick with love's defection.

I went to the coast to hear myself again, to rid my ears of the two opposing voices.

It was eerily light, my cabin filled with the moonlight and the glow of a billion stars.

I dreamed of great waves coming from the sea. Coming over the dunes and washing over the road along the beach.

The morning light was soft and safe. I stepped onto the wet sand, yellow, brown and black. Streaked. Heavy with age. Dolerite stones, tickled by the last gesture of each wave, cackled.

I slipped out of my cotton skin, still creased from a broken sleep, into a frozen awakening. Too cold to drown, too bitter to take the icy liquid into my lungs. My face pointed to the sky, stroking backwards, I swam towards the northern end of the beach. Each breath a gasp as the rippled warning of the coming waves splashed into my mouth and flaring nostrils. Shocked with cold, my ears filled with the sounds of the sea. I heard the dolphin's grey skin sliding through the waves. I heard the shark's hunger.

A large swell broke out of line with the surf and lifted, tossing me in its foam. Like cruel champagne, intoxicating and dangerous, amorous in its hold. I was pushed to the sandy bottom.

'Go on, take a breath if you dare. What are you to me?'

I am a grain of sand. Compressed, imploding. I staggered to my feet and ran back to shore with the weight of the sea against my legs. I lay face down in the sand and felt its grains between my teeth. I rose and walked up a path into a casuarina forest hugging the hillside like soft woolly pills on a worn jumper. I passed through a semicircle of peppermint stumps sunning themselves in sleep, grey grass dancing frenzied at their feet.

Underneath the green-topped casuarinas, the light was tender as dawn as it filtered through the sepia undergrowth. Ground birds and wallabies scurried away to their solitude. Seedpods hugged the boughs. Foliage hung in multiple jointed fingers all about the trees.

'Lie here in this graveyard if you dare. What are you to me?'

I am a tentacle on a casuarina tree.

I lay down on the bed of needles and closed my eyes. I felt my lover's fingers explore my body for its secrets and recalled his desertion. His skin is cold and dead. He is pale and mottled. Dead love surrounds me. He is gone.

A sea eagle's wings beat steadily overhead as it scooped the cliff face. The brown earth breathed through the undergrowth and warmed my skin.

I pushed myself to my feet and made my way over the undergrowth and decaying branches, back towards the open, grassy hill. A wide moat of cutting grass tempted me backwards but I pushed forward. My white skin, splashed with red, numb, insensate. I could only feel my splintered heart.

I broke into a run down the hill, stumbling through the grass. My arms outstretched greeting my dark night and there, through obscurity and torment I fell into an angel's sweet embrace. There, where the sap moves through the casuarinas and the laughter moves the stones.

Fishbone

He chose the restaurant. A warehouse conversion, international cuisine, minimalist decor and beautiful waiters. They were ushered to a centre table. Before the waiter had time to hand them their menus, he ordered seafood platters for two and wine. He was a regular.

They had dated a few times and despite the unseasonal cold, she wore a black strapless dress as he had likened her décolletage to alabaster.

A bottle of pinot gris arrived with an entrée of oysters, shelled and placed on mounds of angel pasta that resembled moss. Lime segments to one side.

After one or two oysters and a short silence, she asked if he'd been to the film festival and he began to praise the latest French release, presuming she had not only seen it but could *parler*, as much of his reply was in French. She had not and could not, but smiled approvingly.

The main course arrived. Prawns and salmon fillets on a mountain of roquette. and they began to eat. Outside, a fog was settling over the city, shrouding the streets, frosting the windows and casting eerie white haloes around the streetlights. A couple entered the restaurant and was shown to a table. The man coached her son's soccer team. She said hello and he walked by without answering. Blushing, she watched them sit down and turned her attention to the waiter who came to ask if they were happy with their meals.

'Yes, fabulous. My compliments to the chef,' she replied when in fact she had not touched her salmon.

'Do you know that man?' he asked and she wondered whom he was addressing as his eyes were fixed on the narrow band of flesh between the waiter's tight jeans and her T-shirt.

'Yes,' she answered, not wanting to bring up her son.

Still lingering, the waiter said she had overheard him speaking French and he boasted of a family chateau in Brittany. She had worked as an au pair in France and claimed to know a little French herself.

Playing with her fish, she peeled the shiny grey skin from its back, exposing its pink flesh, and thought of her lost youth.

'He didn't seem to know you,' he persisted, one eye on the waiter as she moved from table to table.

'*Une autre bouteille, s'il vous plaît,*' he called to her.

She closed her eyes and touched her alabaster chest wishing she could simply disappear. She pictured her empty black dress sitting opposite him. Hovering upright for a minute, the skirt panned elegantly over the chair like a black sail then toppled, the bodice slumped over the fish.

She swallowed a piece of fish and a bone pierced the back of her throat. She coughed into her napkin while he babbled at the waiter as she opened his second bottle. She gulped some wine but the bone was stuck.

'Excuse me,' she spluttered, grabbed her bag and dashed towards the kitchen.

The chef handed her a glass of water and the doughy centre of a bread roll. 'Swallow this whole then drink the water.'

She did as she was told, but the bone was still stuck.

The chef handed her another ball of bread. 'Try again and take a big mouthful of water.'

She swallowed the bread and gulped the water, mascara streaming down her cheeks.

The chef returned to the oven and dished up a small steamed pudding onto a plate and trickled golden syrup over it, garnishing it with a flower and rang the bell for the waiter.

'I think it's out,' she said in a raspy voice.

He wet the end of his apron and gently dabbed her cheeks. They faced each other in silence. Motionless until a shuddered breath fell from her lips.

'Lovely,' he said.

'Thank you,' she stammered, turned and walked away.

She returned to find the waiter clearing the table and her companion gone. She said he had paid and left.

'Where were you?' she asked. 'He thought you'd gone.'

'In the kitchen. Choking on a fishbone.'

'Oh. Perhaps he didn't notice.'

'Perhaps he didn't see me at all,' she said.

Stepping outside, she vanished into the fog.

The Feast of St Francis

'We're going to have a good day,' the nurse says.

'The consummate optimist.'

'There's a special morning tea today.'

'And a harbinger of doom.'

'The local children are bringing in their pets.'

'Your children?'

'Not mine, no.'

'Where are your children?'

'At school. A different one. It's the Feast of St Francis. The children are bringing in some of their pets to show us. Won't that be nice?'

'No, it won't. I'm not going anywhere. Where's my lipstick?'

'Up you get.'

Hauling me to my feet, we enact the same routine with the walking frame.

'Are we walking the course?'

I have ten minutes to check the order, the height and the degree of difficulty. I calculate my horse's strides between each jump and the best angle for approach. She stands at the rail, taking it all in.

'No. Not today. We're walking to the sitting room. Those knees will lock up unless you move. Follow me,' she says.

I never look back when I lead her, so she's sure of my place in the herd. I back her up and walk on again, the reins slack. We do a few hindquarter and forequarter yields to loosen her up then, at the fence, I take her through a right and left side-pass. I saddle and mount her and ride on, tracking her in a large circle then along the arc, turn in. With my weight on my seat bone, my leg on the girth, I shift my other leg behind and flex her. Once she's supple and relaxed, I ride her straight.

'Hold tight.'

'You're pinching me.'

They force me onto this frame oblivious to the fact that every inch of me hurts. I can barely lift these thick-soled shoes. I shuffle and they call it walking, they call it exercise. My arms throb and bruises are spreading from my elbows down to my wrists. I'll be black and blue by the time I reach the sitting room, as my bones are pressed against the metal frame and there's not enough meat on me to bear the strain. I don't know what on earth they've done to my hips. There's something hot inside them. There are spot fires inside me. I'm burning up and my bones are melting.

A fast moving fire ten kilometres wide and thirteen long bears down on property, stock and houses due west of our place. The sky's black and flames leap above an orange horizon. I move the stock by the dam and fill the homestead's gutters. Embers fall from the sky. A change sweeps through. The wind changes direction and the fire turns in on itself and we are spared.

My knees are stiff as a board, my feet are cramping and I can't move.

'My shoes are too tight. I can't ride in these, I'll be disqualified. Where are my boots?'

I spend hours spit and polishing my boots and oiling the saddle and bridle. I wash and dry her blanket, plucking off every dun hair so it's as good a new.

I iron my clean jodhpurs and blouse and hang them on the back of the door. My horse's tack and mine are immaculate and ready to compete.

'They're not tight.'

'I have cramp. I can't bend my toes. They hurt,' I bawl.

'They were fitted by the podiatrist.'

Pod-iat-rist I say inside my head. I can't think for the life of me what that word means. Pod. Peapod. He likes to shell the peas for dinner. Popping the sheaths and flicking the peas into the pot with the tip of his thumb. Podiatrist. She's trying to confuse and distract me from the fire she put inside my hips and the tight shoes she forces me to wear.

My feet feel as though they've been bound and I wriggle and stretch my socked toes and can hear gristle grating inside my joints. I want her to rub them but I don't know her well enough to ask. In fact, I'm not sure I know her at all.

After a hot day in the saddle, horse and rider need a washdown and a rub. I run the hose and sponge over my horse until she's cool then dry every inch of her off with a sweat scraper and check her feet for stones before leading her to her stall. She sighs as I freshen up her water and fill her feedbox with just the right amount of hay, as I don't want her too frisky in the morning. I kiss her cheek goodnight and stroll up the path and onto the veranda. Wrenching off my boots with the boot lever, I stretch my toes then go inside through the laundry door and throw my socks in a bucket of soapy water, hop straight into a hot shower, dress and wait for him to come home to give my feet a rub. He's never too tired for that no matter how hard his day has been.

'Come on. One foot in front of the other. It's easy. Come on, we're meeting the children in the sitting room. Let's not be late for the morning tea.'

'Whose children? Your children?'

'The local children and their pets for the Feast of St Francis.'

'Ah, it hurts,' I bawl, as she urges me on.

'Come on. You're nearly there. Let's sit you down in a nice comfortable chair and you can meet the children and the animals.'

She sits me down in an armchair beside the other inmates. Some of them no more than skeletons cradled in wheelchairs, with wobbly heads and vacant eyes.

'Take me back to my room,' I say when a swarm of children dressed the colour of bees march in single file into the sitting room.

They form a semicircle chattering hundreds of decibels above a buzz. Ripe and clammy from jostling too long in the sun, their excitement is contagious. Some have dogs on leads, others hold rabbits and guinea pigs, one child has a cockatiel perched on her shoulder. Strawberry-blonde hair falls in curls.

A teacher nods and the children fall silent then burst into song.

All things bright and beautiful

I know that tune, those words. I've heard them before.

All creatures great and small…each little flower that opens, each little bird that sings…

I hear myself singing and a mob of Merinos swoon.

God made their glowing colours and made their tiny wings

A small dog begins to howl and the children giggle.

'Chippie. Traitor. You're supposed to help me bring them in. Chippie. Useless,' I shout and a little boy lets out a hoot.

His face colours as my eyes meet his and he seals his lips but his cheeks bloat with stifled laughter.

'Come back, you bastard.'

The dog whimpers.

'Quiet. You'll upset the children.'

'Bastard,' I scream and with what little strength I have left, project myself out of my chair and lunge at her.

My ears ring like church bells and I topple and crash to the floor, my legs tangled in the walking frame then splayed on the linoleum with my skirt up around my pants. My tissue-thin skin breaks and blood sluices from my thigh and shin. A burning pain shoots up my side.

A dozen pairs of children's eyes widen and the curse I had in mind becomes a drooling slur.

Cracker Night

It was Sydney's last legal cracker night. A cold one. Cloudless, nothing but God's stars splattered across the sky and a hint of a new moon. Misted breath puffed from our mouths. Our skin rose in gooseflesh and we shivered, not caring as each of us held a sparkler spitting spangled lights and curling red hot. We made patterns. Circles and spirals. The letters of our names.

We were rugged up in the greasy wool cardigans and beanies our grandma had knitted. Each one a different coloured wool. Dad had carefully laid out the fireworks in order of their firing on Mum's best silver drinks tray, despite her protest. She stood by the door as she didn't like the cold or the throwdowns we aimed at her feet.

Dad, as always, was master of ceremonies. Lighting a Roman candle first was the family tradition and we all cooed at its colourful glory and squealed at its exploding shells.

Then he lit a few tuppenny bungers and threw them across the courtyard and they banged loudly.

'I'll save the rest for that blasted owl,' he laughed.

He was a light sleeper and our resident boobook drove him to distraction. He was often seen running up the hallway and hurling a lit bunger out the second-storey window in the dead of night. 'Boom' then silence and fifteen minutes later the double hoot would sound again until dawn.

'Next the Catherine wheel,' Dad announced.

Its spiral tube was mounted on a stand higher than Dad himself. Once ignited, it spun and hissed, shooting sparks and silver flames. The faster it spun, the louder we clapped and cooed. Its stand began to rattle

and wobble wildly on the tray and in a shower of spilling sparks, it toppled over igniting everything in its path.

Flaming shooting stars and flaring rockets shot across the courtyard,
between our legs, over our heads and off through the railing into the
garden. tuppenny bungers went off in a deafening staccato.

Mum jumped inside, screeching unintelligibly. I followed smartly
while my brother roared with laughter, revelling in the bedlam.

Flames, flares, sparks and explosions all around him, Dad hitched up
his trousers and began leaping about, frantically dodging the rockets.

I peered out the window, a madman dancing an Irish gig.

The Mummy Pavilion

I had promised to take her to the Royal Easter Show to see the animals.

Rising early, she dressed in her favourite blue velvet dress and scuffed leather shoes. Worn through paddock and bog, but still her best. When I held out her jeans and gumboots instead, she folded her arms and stamped her foot, and reminded me that it was her treat – her day. I conceded with the proviso that her favourite Barbie doll stayed home.

'But she's all dressed in her new pink and white spotty dress,' she whined, but accustomed to a bargain she tucked the doll into bed.

It was a dark grey day. The air damp with drizzle. The colours of the show lit the low clouds in moving prisms. Fairground music filled the air. My little girl's eyes widened in wonder and she gripped my hand as we walked with the crowd through the turnstile.

'I want to see the chooks,' she called.

We stopped while I scanned the map.

'The chooks, the chooks,' she chanted.

Collecting the eggs had been her first and a much-loved chore. Each morning and in all weathers, she would make her way to the coop and return with two brown eggs in the palms of her outstretched hands.

I found the pavilion on the map and we wove through the crowd, hand in hand. The smell reached us first. Pungent, bucolic.

As we entered, I pointed to the desk by the front door and explained that if we were separated, that was where she was to go. 'Do you understand?' I asked through the cacophony of people and poultry.

I didn't hear her reply. My eyes were drawn like magnets to the long corridors of cages were filled with exotic fowl. A red-feathered, black-tailed Phoenix stood proud and tall in his enclosure, head raised, crowing loudly. A peep of small fluffy white Silkies nested quietly next to a great Sultan, mysterious with his white plume covering his face. A green-black-feathered Minorca stood with the elegant stance of a bull-fighter. His wattles lurid. His comb erect and proud.

'Oh my,' I said, utterly transfixed. I stared dreamily into his eye.

He strutted on the spot, drumming the floor and puffing out his chest. A Hemingway bird.

Turning to my daughter, I pointed at him, but she wasn't there. I called her name. No answer. My worst fear surged through me. I called her name again, my voice ragged with panic. People agog.

The Minorca crowed and drummed wildly in reply.

I called for her again and again through my constricting throat. Then I heard the loudspeaker announce a lost child and my burning body cooled. Raising the sawdust, I ran towards the desk and saw her.

'Thank you so much,' I said to the attendant who, on seeing me, held my daughter's hand and drew her close.

'Are you her mother?'

'Yes.'

'Are you sure?' she asked running her eyes from my hair down my jeans to my dusty Blundstone boots.

I felt myself flush.

'I beg your pardon?'

'You don't fit the description,' she said, looking back at my child. 'High heels, a pink and white spotted dress and a blonde ponytail.'

'Come on,' I said and took my daughter's hand and pulled her away.

We stood for a moment outside the pavilion and let the drizzle cast its beads over our hair and shoulders like dew on a web. I squatted down beside her and looked into her eyes. I wanted to slap her. From panic. From relief.

'Why did you say that?' I asked.

A smile lit her face. 'It's the mummy I wanted you to be.'

The Sweet Taste of Yabby

Mother cried an ocean and Dad's solution: a seaside holiday. We had never taken a holiday before and I had never seen the sea. Our place was seven hundred kilometres inland. I was abuzz with excitement.

The doctor prescribed Mother a hospital spell but Dad knew better. He always knew best.

'Sea air in her lungs and bare feet in the sand, she'll come right,' he said.

The doctor disagreed.

'A change of scenery is what she needs, not doctors and nurses, people she doesn't know.'

The station hand moved into the house to keep an eye on things while we were away. The lambs were already weaned, drenched and vaccinated and were out fattening up on the best pasture. Dad had jetted the ewes and culled the broken mouths, dry and doggy ones. We could afford a short break to see Mother well again.

We left the Western Plains behind on a night as black as Mother's mood and drove the long stretch of the Gwydir Highway. I snuggled underneath a crocheted rug, stretching out and dozing on the backseat, which was all my own.

Through the rear window, I watched the sky for the first light of dawn, which never seemed to come. 'Are we there yet?' I asked repeatedly until finally I saw the sun's firstborn rays.

'Look at that sunrise,' Dad exclaimed, and still Mother cried.

We pulled over and Dad and I jumped out of the car and stared wide-eyed at what looked like the very end of the earth. Science had got it all wrong and the earth was flat. Our place was dead flat, not a landmark in sight, and the sea was obviously the end.

Waves surged and broke, churning the white sand along the shore. There were a few early surfers catching a dawn ride, carving the swell.

'Come and look.' I turned and called to Mother but she didn't look up. Her face was buried in her hands.

We checked into a family room in a beachfront motel and Mother took straight to her bed and didn't raise her head from the pillow for the whole week no matter what we said or did. Dad made her cups of tea, which sat on the bedside table, turning that nasty grey they do when cold. He spoke to her in whispers, running his hands through her hair. Still she didn't rise.

We ate fish and chips every night perched on the edge of her bed, opening the newspaper like a game of pass the parcel.

'You must eat,' Dad said to her, and she grimaced, lacing her fingers together, squeezing them until they turned white.

I wolfed down handfuls of hot salty chips, hidden behind Dad's back lest I catch Mother's scathing eye.

After dinner, I crept away early to bed. My bedding was clean and crisp. The hospital corners so tight could barely get in. There were two pillows, soft and plump and the air puffed out of them in a 'pshhhh' as I laid my head down. At night, the wind rattled the windows and thunder rumbled out to sea. I slept soundly with the storm and the pounding waves a lullaby.

In the morning, the sun slunk back out of the sea to the sound of cicada song and Mother's muted cries.

'Coming for a a dip?' Dad asked, sporting a pair of Okanuis, his bandy legs and chest nearly as white as the sand, his forearms dark brown.

'Yes, I am,' I said, wriggling into bathers and pulling on a sunhat.

Outside, frangipani perfume filled the air. The bitumen road was near melting and burned our feet, so we hopped into the gutter and walked single file to the beach. The sand burned too, so we dumped our towels and hopped to the water's edge to cool our feet.

The beach was dotted with coloured umbrellas, beach towels and more people than the crowd at the district show. The sand moved underfoot with the push and pull of the waves. The shore was littered with worm hollows and tiny shells, some pure white with holes for threading and others are streaked gold and brown.

I thought I'd make a necklace for Connie. I said her name out loud and something broke inside my chest.

Dad leapt in the water, diving through the break and swimming out beyond it. He flipped over onto his back and floated while I dithered at the edge, collecting shells and lying on my belly while the ocean bubbled over me. A rogue shore break gripped me and I tumbled in its arms before it threw me back onto the sand. Staggering to my feet, I emptied my bathers of sand and stood in the shallows watching my sunhat float away.

'My hat, my hat,' I hollered until Dad swam back to shore.

'Shhh, Bella. We'll get you another one in town,' he said, and we stood hand-in-hand watching my hat drift out to sea.

'The sea sure is is something, isn't it?' he said, breaking the spell.

Salt dried in patterns on our skin.

'There are shells with holes. I'm going to make Connie a necklace.'

I heard him gasp and we stood in silence, our eyes fixed on the rutted horizon. He squeezed my hand so hard thought my bones would break and I was glad of the pain.

Reeds rise out of the brown dam like sentinels, their edges razor-sharp, their tips a bearskin hat. Silky soft mud oozes between our bare toes. We know there are eels in the dam, as their slimy bodies brush against our legs and slither around our ankles. We hate them, Connie and me, but there are also yabbies in that murky, squirming dam, which is why we go in. Nothing beats yabbying.

Mother stuffs her old stockings with meat. She wears stockings and skirts even on the farm. Dad tells her to wear trousers but she stubbornly refuses. She's never worn them in her life and she's not about to start now. Dad gives her trousers every birthday, which always makes her laugh, as she knows something special will be hidden in the pocket. She searches for her treasure and, finding it, kisses him on the top of his balding head, which she calls his 'fly rink'. They titter and hug and we wonder how the same joke year after year can be SO funny.

The way we see it, Connie and me, thistles and burrs soon see a lustrous tan leg laddered and Mother's stockings provide an endless supply of yabby traps. Silky, tan yappy traps.

Mother hands us a stocking each stuffed with slices of raw mutton. Connie also takes a brown paper bag filled with biscuits and I take a a tin bucket filled with ice. Made sleepy by the cold, yabbies on ice are easier to handle, Mother says. The day is a scorcher and the ice will melt in no time but Mother insists on it and there's no arguing with her. We do as she says and bolt the front door and push our feet into our boots. We'd do anything to go yabbying. The bucket handle squeaks as it swings back and forth beating my calf as I run to the dam. Connie's at my heels.

'I dare you to go in first,' I say as we kick off our boots and Connie starts to whimper. 'Chicken!'

I stride into the dam and she follows.

In no time, blue claws attach themselves to my bloody meat stocking.

'Got ya,' I cry, hauling my catch through the mud to shore and into the bucket. I peer in and shout, 'It's huge!'

It lashes the bucket nearly upending it.

'The biggest ever!'

Leaving my boots where I left them, I run home, dodging thistles, stones and burrs.

Bursting through the door, I call to Mother, who answers from the kitchen where she's kneading bread dough on the bench, her hands white with flour.

'Look what I caught. It's a monster!'

She washes her hands and heats a large pot of water to the boil and we drop in the yabby and watch it thrash, redden and die.

'What a beauty, Bella,' she says. 'Come and see, Connie,' she calls while I dance around her legs, beaming.

No one comes. No one answers.

'Connie?'

Turning to me with her pretty face vehement, she shouts, 'Where's Connie? You're supposed to be watching her."

I turn off the stove and pluck the yabby from the pot and plunge it into a bowl of cold water while Mother bolts, slamming the screen door behind her. She's still wearing her apron. It's blue gingham with a white frilled pocket and a a bow tied at the back.

While the yabby cools, I quarter a lemon, as its juices offset the muddy taste. I break the yabby shell with the back of a knife and peel it back. As my mouth waters, I squeeze the lemon over the flesh and sprinkle a pinch of salt onto the meat and take my first bite.

In the distance, I can hear Mother wailing like a birthing cow and gulp it down. Turning, I reach for one more morsel and chew it slowly, rolling it around my tongue, so it reaches every taste bud.

Then I go back to the dam. Mother has waded in fully clothed and an air bubble has formed under her apron. It balloons around her waist. I look around the bank for her shoes but they are nowhere to be seen. She must have worn them in and they will be covered in mud and I laugh.

Connie is lying face down in the water, tendrils of her strawberry-blonde hair floating about her. Mother turns her over and her face is white and her lips are violet. Her hands bob to the surface, her little puckered fingers curled over her palms. Her legs, a tangle of weeds.

Mother's mouth gapes and twists. 'Jim,' she screams. Her rasping cry rings across the farm.

Sheep start and scamper away. The dogs yelp. Dad turns, drops his fencing tools and wire and runs towards the dam, his great big boots thumping the earth.

Mother's body is bent in two as she cradles Connie in her arms.

Dad splashes into the dam, boots and all as well. He wraps his arms around Mother and Connie and hauls them both back onto the bank. Laying Connie on the ground, he turns her on her side and water slops out of her mouth. Then he turns her on her back and thumps her chest then pushes it with linked hands and breathes into her mouth. Again and again and again.

Mother screams, 'She's gone. She's gone.'

She can't be gone, I think. She's my baby sister. 'Make her come back,' I scream.

Dad pushes her chest and blows until he's out of breath and slumps on the ground.

'Daddy?'

My whole world sinks. My stomach plunges into my bowels and something grips it like a a vice. A cold and heavy weight swallows my childhood. Shock's dreadful chill fills my legs, fusing me to the bank. Connie is dead and it's my fault. I killed my baby sister.

Mother falls into Dad's arms and together they kneel before the dead body of their child, drenched, howling, keening.

I stand alone, with nothing but the sweet taste of yabby in my mouth.

'Come on, Bella. Let's get you a new hat and a a bite to eat,' Dad said.

We picked up our towels, shook off the sand and threw them around our necks. We walked the length of the beach, popping dried bluebottles with our heels, their sting long gone.

Writing my name in the wet sand, I watched the sea wash it away.

I wanted to write her name, 'Connie', but I couldn't bear the thought of it disappearing.

The Planter

Dinner heralded an armistice between father and son, a welcome respite from their well-worn argument. Imploring his father to diversify only fell on deaf ears.

'My father and his father before him were sheep men, not croppers. Look around you. Everything we have is from wool.'

'Wool's finished, Dad.'

'It'll come back. We've had hard times before. We'll get through. We always have. It's in our blood.'

Blood had the last word.

Jean called for Libby's return.

'I can't just drop things here, Mum.'

A daughter would never inherit property. It would go to Jim, the only son. Libby moved to Sydney, secured a job and rented a small but tidy flat.

'I need you home,' Jean repeated.

'I live here, Mum. I have a job. A flat. I can't just come home.'

'Dad's shooting the sheep and Jim's ploughing up the paddocks.'

'Christ!'

Libby requested leave, half hoping her manager would say no.

'You have a huge amount of leave, not to mention long service. Go home. Your job will be waiting for you. No one is indispensable, others will step up,' she said.

Early the next morning, she drove nine hours nor'-west. As the minutes ticked by, the temperature rose and the country levelled out, she felt a weight she hadn't known was there drop off her shoulders.

Turning at the homestead's sign, she bumped the along the corrugated dirt road, avoiding potholes, rabbits and the odd roo. Immense paddocks dotted with sheep, bimble box and coolabahs stretched before her. She pulled up at the homestead; its silver roof glinted the warmth of home.

Greeted with an uncharacteristically awkward hello, her father picked up her bag and took it to her room and disappeared into his study.

A pair of dogs curled up on an old couch blinked open their eyes and beat their tails on the cushions; they were not moving for anyone. They had pride of place and marked their territory with moulted hair. Jim was already asleep.

Jean had prepared plate of cold meat and salad, which was waiting in the kitchen. 'Men have lost their place. Their farms are failing. They're shooting the sheep and they don't talk to anyone. Just hold it all inside and we women folk can do nothing but watch them fall over,' she said.

'Not Dad, though.'

'Do you know how tiring it is trying to buoy him? I fuss over him, cook, clean, and rub his feet. I act the fool to raise a smile when the last thing I feel like doing is clowning around. Honestly, if anyone saw me, they would have me locked up. And why? Why do I do it? Because I'm terrified I'll find him hanging in the shed one day.' Jean fixed her eyes on the wall and her mouth dried with dread at the very thought of it.

Lost for words and too tired to take it all in, Libby rinsed her plate, kissed her mother goodnight and headed for bed. She stripped off and sank into her soft mattress. Around the room were trinkets from her childhood: a collection of ceramic horses, a box of cards and books jammed higgledy-piggledy into a wooden shelf. Old clothes hung in the wardrobe and spilled out of the drawers.

Her mind drifted to what her mother had said and she wondered if she was thinking of leaving. 'Christ,' she said, and drifted into a deep sleep, dreaming of bitumen and blurred golden-brown landscape.

Sunrise streamed through open curtains. Libby pulled on her work clothes and made her way onto the veranda.

Her father was in the yard mounting his horse, brushing a swarm of flies.

Libby saw his hand tremble. 'You okay, Dad?' she called.

He didn't reply, so she hurried down the steps, dodging the bindi-eyes on lawn.

She climbed the rail and asked again, 'You okay?'

He turned and thought for a moment and called for the dogs, broke into a slow trot and headed east. Libby watched them until they swayed and blurred into a mirage and vanished.

Jim pushed open the screen door. 'Reckon you could bring the ewes in from the south to the house paddock today? We can set stock them from there.'

'Where are the rams?'

'You can get what's left of them tomorrow and we'll join the best of them. Dad's got the wethers and a mob of ewes in the yards. There's a truck coming if he doesn't shoot them first.'

Her horse was waiting with her head hung over the fence, ears pricked and nickering. It had been months since Libby had been home but it was still there, the bond between them. She didn't have to catch her, she simply opened the gate and she trotted in. As she saddled and mounted her, she looked out towards a pall of tractor dust.

At the far end of the south paddock, a mob of ewes were grazing by the fence. The air smelled of lanolin and sheep shit. Libby felt a pang inside her chest, a deep sense of belonging.

The sheep raised their heads and scampered off, splitting into two groups. Libby joined them back into one mob then walked them on, pushing them slowly along the dappled shadows to the dam. They clattered over the bank and drank, pushing and shoving each other, as the water was low. The cracked bank radiated heat, begging for rain.

Squinting towards the sun, Libby's face was already clammy and her head drenched. She flipped off her hat and fanned herself. She leaned forward and lay across her mare's neck listening to the clatter of hoofs, the whine of flies and the swish of her tail.

No traffic, trains, music or chatter. It was bliss.

She sat up and hooted, the sheep flinched. One of the ewes started to trot around the dam and the others followed. Round and round they went, bleating and scuttling until one broke the circle. It was their way, their pattern, the only thing for it was patience, and out there, Libby had all the time in the world to wait them out.

Pushing them into the home paddock, she was satisfied that she had not missed even one.

Jean was waiting on the veranda, wringing her hands strangely. 'Dad didn't come home for lunch,' she said.

'Maybe he took it with him.'

'He couldn't boil an egg, you know that. I'm worried.'

'He'll be right.'

'Something's wrong. I can feel it.'

Evening dyed the country pink and mauve and somewhere out of the pastel light came a riderless chestnut, his saddle askew and his eyes wild. One dog trotted after him, coat full of burrs.

'I'll take the vehicle out. Maybe there's a fence down. Or the truck broke down. Or… I'll go and look,' Jim said.

Jean uttered a strangled cry from the back of her throat.

'Come on, Mum.'

The next morning, Jim and Libby rode eastward.

They scanned the expanse. Ordinarily, they loved the place, its searing hot summers, its solitude and the flat-as-a-strap paddocks. Generations of her family had lived out there and each one of them loved every paddock, tree and cutting scrub on the place. It was as though they owned the land all the way to the end of the earth and the very best part of it. The best-kept secret. Most people lived out their lives clustered around the seaboard or perched on a mountain and Libby's family were happy to keep it that way. The big country was theirs. Now it seemed vast and desolate, like a foreign land.

'Look!'

'It's a roly-poly.'

'I don't think so.'

They cantered towards it and Libby took a flying dismount and picked it up.

'Dad's hat. It's Dad's hat,' she called, swinging it about in mid-air. She looked around frantically, calling 'Dad, Dad.'

Then she saw a trail of broken grass and her father lying face down beneath a cloud of bottle green flies. Hector sat beside him whimpering.

Libby ran to his side and thought she saw him move. 'He's alive!' she called, even though the putrid stench of death filled the air. They knew that smell well out there but Libby refused to believe it.

She knelt down. 'Dad?'

Rolling him onto his back, she saw his face, cut and grazed, congealed blood clinging to his hair. His eyes were wide open and glassy. Meat ants feasted on his flesh.

Jim retched then spat, turned and galloped towards the homestead.

Libby sat cross-legged beside her father's lifeless body and covered his face with his Planter.

She gathered clumps of dirt and held it in her clenched fists while the grass swayed around her.

With These We Will Never Go Hungry

There must be a mistake. The reflection in the mirror is that of an old woman. Stooped. Snow-white hair. Canyons etched into a gaunt face. Sallow skin flecked with brown liver spots. Stagnant brown eyes beneath a milky film. Poor old dear doesn't look at all well.

A tremulous voice breaks through her thin lips. 'Where's my lipstick?'

The room in which she sits is small. The walls are painted peach and the floor lined with grey linoleum. The furniture rudimentary. A bed, a chair and a mirrored dressing table. There's a sash window overlooking a garden and a slow-moving river. A mountain range in the distance. There's a still life in a gaudy frame hanging on the wall. Flowers in a vase. Its perspective skewed.

Nurses strip me bare and I stand before them, presenting a pair of shrivelled breasts and a sagging stomach. There is no room here for modesty, they say. There's always room for modesty, I reply, and they snigger as they dry me with a scratchy towel.

Humiliation the spirit-breaker of choice.

'I want to go home.'

How I long for a soak in the hot springs.

At home, there wasn't another soul for miles around in the big country. There was room to breathe. Nothing but red earth and sky. No intruders. Only wide-open solitude.

The ute bumped along the corrugated road to the spring. Cutting the engine and the lights, I'd get out, strip and leave my clothes on the bonnet and stand naked before a lowing herd of cattle. The moon shone on my skin. The waters of the Great Artesian Basin bubbled to the surface of a concrete tank. I'd perch on the edge, acclimatising my feet and legs to the hot water before slipping in up to my neck. My body would turn lobster pink. Steam would condense on my face, cleansing the day's dirt. I'd sing and the herd of love-struck Poll Hereford's knees would buckle at the sound of my voice.

Far off, the homestead lights flickered in the darkness like a tiny cluster of stars. Strange how lights flicker; I've never known why. In my mind, I see him sitting in his favourite chair reading the newspaper, moaning about the weather, the state of the country and falling beef prices and the dog at his feet concurring with a beating tail. He would drain a glass of rum and his temper would begin fray. The dog would beat a hasty retreat lest he catch the end of his boot.

I cower down into the spring until the water touches my bottom lip, which has begun to tremble at the thought of him.

'Arms up.'

I lift my arms above my head like I'm under arrest; they're so heavy my shoulders begin to quake. The nurses fumble with my nightgown and it gets stuck on my head.

'I can't breathe.'

They tug it hard, scratching the bridge of my nose. My spent arms fall down by my side and bounce against my hipbones. There'll be bruises on my wrists. Soon my skin will be aubergine.

'My nose!'

'Just a little scratch, sweetheart,' she says, pulling a pair of oversized underpants up my legs and pushing a thick pad into the gusset. Sweetheart indeed!

'It's Mrs…'

I can't remember names, not even my own.

'It's Mrs to you!'

She dabs my nose with an alcohol wipe and it stings.

'Get that off me!'

I fall back onto the bed and glare at her. Coral lipstick bleeds into the lines and cracks around her mouth. I know that colour. It's mine!

'You! Give it back!'

I watch her cheek twitch and hear her teeth tap faintly. She lifts my legs and shuffles them beneath the sheets. Tap, tap, clatter. An impatient tic.

'You stole my lipstick!'

She clicks her tongue. Tsk, tsk, tsk. I know that sound.

My skin rises into gooseflesh and I shiver.

'Chilly? Someone walk over your grave?' she asks.

I nod and they cover me with a blanket, talking over the top of me as though I'm not here.

'Had four days off.'

'Go anywhere?'

'Home.'

They pull the bedspread up to my chin and fold it back in perfect symmetry with the sheet line and tuck it in at the sides.

'Nice. What'd you get up to?'

'Not much. Podded broad beans with Mum.'

'Borin'!'

'Don't you complain! Those are the year's greens,' I interject, but she doesn't seem to hear me.

I spent days clearing thistles, weeds and a few raggedy self-seeded vegetables from the garden bed near the house. The red dirt was as hard as stone. It had been that long since it had been turned, let alone watered. I soaked it with the watering cans I'd carried up from the dam. I turned the soil and marked out the bed from the patchy weed infested lawn with a line of old bricks. Nettles stuck to my arms and my skin blistered. Still, I persisted, determined to please and bring back the spark in his eye and his killing smile with a homely garden, a productive nest. The rest of the garden was a shambles save a few saltbushes and a leggy damask rose. The rose was out of place and I wondered who planted it. I knew nothing of the place's history. His history. His people. And I knew not to ask. 'One bed at a time,' I said to myself, trying not to think of the housework awaiting me. I dug in some chook manure and then made mounds in tidy rows. I planted herbs seedlings and vegetable seeds and ran water along the canals. I marked each row with a stake and tied on a name tag. I fenced off the bed with wire, which I dug deep into the ground, as the rabbits were in plague proportions. Tools down, I admired my work before gathering the weeds into the wheelbarrow.

Across the sheds, I heard him grumbling, exasperated by the broken-down tractor.

'You could call the neighbour,' I called. 'He can fix anything.'

He strode towards me and his silence crumbled my smile. Fists clenched he stood over me and snarled, 'Can he now?' and I knew I'd said the wrong thing and waited for the back of his hand.

'Mrs…'

I can't think of his name. My name. Names, parts of the day and my lipstick have gone missing. There's much that's gone and much I try to forget.

'Fed up with the sight of broad beans,' the nurse says.

I wonder momentarily if I'm invisible, as they chat to each other and fuss over the corners of bed and the line of the bedspread against the sheet fold. I check myself with a soft pinch on the arm – yes, still here.

'I am here, you know, and it's rude to talk over the top of someone.'

Their arms linked through mine, they haul me up onto a pile of plumped pillows. Plastic crackles beneath me. A bib is fixed around my neck.

Indignity the spirit-breaker of choice.

There's movement outside my door and I hear rattling in the corridor. It must be suppertime. I wonder what delight will be on my tray. Mush for the gummy residents. Unpalatable slop. They're starving us. Some of them in here are as thin as fledglings, cradled in sheepskin and spoon-fed. Others are craggy old men and women. Heads bent over their bowls, slurping and gurgling. Drinking tea from beakers, their juddering hands incapable of holding a cup and their ill-fitting teeth clicking and clacking against the crockery.

'Drove into town. Still know everyone there and they know every-one else's business. Pack of sticky beaks.'

'One café and guess what they serve? Instant coffee!'

'Gross.'

'Nothin' ever happens there.'

'Noth-ing,' I say.

'It's so bloody borin-g.'

The corners of her mouth twists into a smirk.

'He who seeks rest finds boredom. He who seeks work finds rest,' I say and they tuck in the bedspread so tight I can hardly breathe.

'That's one way of keeping me quiet,' I heave.

'Then this car screeches to a halt and a fella jumps out, shouting. "Help! Call an ambulance! Somebody help!" I run out and tell him I'm a nurse.'

'There's a dead man in the bushes. Back there. Call an ambulance. He says, all red in the face. The waitress says she'll call and I run up the road lookin' everywhere for the dead bloke.'

'Oh my God,' the other nurse says.

'I saw him wrigglin' in the blackberry. The local drunk. Harmless enough. They reckon he and his wife come from Germany after World War II to start over. She died soon after arrivin' but and he started hittin' the bottle. Cancel that ambulance, I say. It's just Mick. I pulled him out and he's all bloody and bruised. Asked him how long he's been in there and he says, "Best part of the day."'

The other nurse snorts.

'He smelled rotten and I told him I'd call the doctor but he wouldn't hear of that so I walked him home and he kept stoppin' and sayin' "You're bloody beautiful you are. Beautiful." Enough rum on his breath to get me pissed.'

I know that smell. Rum breath in my face. On my tongue. Sweet, burning rum. I shudder.

'I've made a vegetable patch,' I said, gesturing to the garden, waiting for a word of praise, just one.

His sealed lips turned down at the corners. He bent down to the wheelbarrow and pulled out a lone broad bean seedling and shook his head and clicked his tongue thrice. Tsk, tsk, tsk.

'These are the year's greens. With these, we will never go hungry.'

'I planted broad bean seeds.'

'I've told you before not to waste!' he barked, throwing the seedling my feet. 'Plant it!'

'But…'

He struck my face so hard I was momentarily blinded. I cried out and he slammed my nose with the heel of his palm, splitting my philtrum. I tried to fend him off and he laughed. I dropped to my knees and started to crawl across the lawn. Thorns pierced my hands and stones bruised my knees as I crawled. I groped the ground in search of the garden bed to guide me to the path, to the backdoor, inside. I'd been blinded before. I'd crawled before. I was trying to get to the bathroom. To the one door with a lock. His breathing quickened and the earth groaned under his stride. I felt myself lifted and was carried inside. My nose dripping blood. I could barely breathe. The screen door slammed behind us and I began to tremble. I knew what was coming. He threw me on the sofa, rolled me over and jammed my face into the cushions. He tore at my underclothes, parted my legs and drove himself deep inside me, then fell away moaning.

I shudder.

'Need another blanket?'

I shake my head.

'So I get to his cottage and all the windows are boarded up and the paint's peelin' off and he tells me I can't come in cos it's "unfit for visitors". I go in anyway. Empty flagons and dirty dishes everywhere. And one big chair. He's staggerin' all over the place, so I sit him down, get some water and clean him up a bit. Then I saw all them books. Poetry books. Leather-bound. Fancy.'

'Poetry? What happened then?' the other nurse asks.

'I asked him to read me a poem and he threw me out.'

'Bloody funny.'

I look up at her and say, 'Nothing ever happens?'

She looks at me, puzzled 'What?'

'You said nothing ever happens there. Doesn't sound like it.'

'He who seeks rest finds boredom. He who seeks work finds rest,' she says to me smugly.

A blue-uniformed woman bursts into the room, smacking a tray down on my dresser. I can't take my eyes off her gaping buttons, wondering when they will burst free and fly off the front of her dress. The uniforms here are different shades of blue. The nurses wear navy. The cooks and the cleaners pale blue. The paler the blue, the lower the station. The paler the blue, the further the mountain.

One of the nurses butters a slice of white bread then scoops some soup into a spoon, blows on it and lifts it to my mouth.

'What is it?'

'Bean soup.'

'With these, we will never go hungry.'

Nor'-west

I loomed large amid a swarm of children barracking for their team at the inter-school carnival. Ripe and clammy from too long in the sun, their excitement was palpable. Wafting across the field, the smell of a sausage sizzle.

I moved to the track rail to watch my child sprinting five metres ahead of her opponents, her hair streaming behind her like a flag.

'She flies.'

I turned to see a little boy standing beside me, his smile broad.

My child tore through the finish line then stopped and stooped over her knees to catch her breath. Standing, she beamed as an official pinned another blue ribbon to her T-shirt.

'She does,' I answered.

The boy glanced back to his mother, who was sitting in the grandstand. Her eyes never left him. The memory of being pulled from the arms of her mother still raged inside her. Her mother's screams still filled her head. Taken and raised by strangers. Taken from her mother. From her people. Pushed into a starched dress, her bare feet trapped in lace-trimmed socks and tight black leather shoes. The scar on her heart ached as she watched her son share just two words.

The children cheered as another winner crossed the line. My pink-cheeked child ran up ribbons flapping about her T-shirt like. She pulled the arm of the boy and together they ran off into the nearby paddock. Kicking off their shoes. Playing barefoot until the dirt clung to their ankles.

The leaden sky was streaked pink and orange as we drove home along the long dirt road, too weary to recount the day. A storm was building on the horizon. Late in the night, from the comfort of my bed, I woke to the sound of rain smacking the iron roof. There'd be a crop this year. An income.

The morning sun burst through the scattered remnants of storm clouds and news of an accident crackled over the radio. The driver and passenger of a blue sedan killed by a speeding truck. I froze as I heard their names. The boy and his mother.

There were no words to explain death to my child not yet ten years old. Over the next week, I watched her grieve, sorrow shading her eyes.

Together, we walked across the cemetery towards two new graves in a place too lonely for one so young. I watched the muscles along her jaw clench and twitch like those of an old man. I heard her say goodbye. A bunch of flowers wilted in her fist. Then I placed my hand gently on her shoulder and ushered her towards the car and drove her home.

I watched her back as she stood with her face pressed against the window. She stared out into the garden where the boy, drenched by the garden sprinkler, had once climbed the box gum. Her breath formed a circle on the glass. With one finger, she wrote his initials in the condensation.

She breathed him in and out. Listening for his voice, watching for his shadow as the wind picked up the leaves and danced them lonely in the air.

The Atoll

The currawongs' place is wild. Soaring above the mountain, they see everything. Mt Wellington's ethereal secrets. Clouds hastening overhead. The river. The sea. Gulls playing about yachts, swooping and diving, hovering on the updraft. Sailors with one eye on the weather knowing how quickly the change from calm to a gale. The city below sprawled like a sleeping seal. The perpetual feast of mice, insects, carrion and heath berries. Further down the southern slopes, orchards and chicken coops, ripe for the picking. Dark wooded ranges beyond. Islands off the island. Mountains. Bruny's Mt Mangana, its skirt a rainforest. Maria's Mt Maria, capped by dolerite columns. The woman with whom they share their place is also an island. A loner, an aesthete, a sensitive.

The ruckus they made was plain. A warning so loud, thirty or more currawongs came down from the mountain to see what the fuss was all about, hopeful of a feed. They too sensed imminent danger and lined up along the wires of the hills hoist, joining in a loud chorus of 'kar-week-week-kar' but the woman took no notice.

It was common enough for them to hold a raucous party in her garden. Methodical birds were afforded playtime and one of their favourite sports was to see how many pegs they could pull from her peg basket and scatter them along the lawn. This was no mean feat. They would hang upside down and slide open the basket latch, lift the lid then throw the pegs one at a time. All the birds cheering and laughing from the grandstand.

This was different. This was no game.

One flew down to the windowsill and pecked at the glass but it was too late.

Perched on the edge of a stool at her desk, her feet evenly placed along the foot-rail, her gold-rimmed glasses pushed up into her hair, she examined a yellow grevillea style through a microscope. What she saw, she would translate masterfully onto the page. Stroke by stroke. Mark by mark.

Dissected plants, pens and pencils arranged on the window ledge according to their height. A stack of fine paper in a dust jacket. A chest of artist drawers bulging with botanical illustrations and herbarium boards. Wall to ceiling shelves stacked with plant specimens preserved in formaldehyde. A bookcase held a variety of scientific texts and journals in which she had been published. Wrap-around windows gave her maximum natural light and a view of her beloved garden but still, a bright light hung overhead. There was always a cup of tea on the go, greying as cooled.

As a child, she wandered the mountain's paths and tracks, sketching plants. The mountain gave her all she needed; it was her playground, her teacher and her friend, and now it earned her a modest living.

Her cottage was built on the foundations of her childhood home, which was razed in an immense bushfire. Situated just about as high on Mount Wellington as a house could be, it was as far away from any other people as possible. Whether she lived there because she always had or for peace and quiet, no one knew. There would have been little of the latter given the mountain's howling wind.

If there was a ray of sunshine, she lunched on a cushioned wicker chair in her garden. Sometimes, her glasses caught the sun, sending prisms of refracted light into the trees, which was always of great interest to a passing forest raven. At the first sound of a car on the nearby road, or even worse the cooee of the gregarious postman, she would scurry back indoors like the long-tailed mouse down its burrow.

Spring had arrived and, with it, a hundred jonquils were pushing their heads up through the mossy excuse for a lawn. Any grass had little hope against the voracious paddymelons. Hardy snowdrops were already in flower, as were the rhododendrons in pinks, whites and deep purples. There were territories to stake out and mates to find and all the mountain birds were in full, feverish song. The golden whistlers exclaimed with a crack after every phrase. The scarlet robins sang sweetly. The spectral cry of the black cockatoo rang out over the mountain and through the valley below, the harbinger of rain.

A knock on the door made her jump and there, standing on her doormat, was a man with all the stealth of a cat and the low of a masked owl. A fellow illustrator had come to see her work so she ushered him into her studio. Flipping through her drawings, he nodded and shrugged and occasionally lifted one corner of his mouth. He showed her his sketchbook and complained about how women had taken over the publishing industry and a middle-aged man struggled to win commissions.

After a long pause, she began to tell him about the bushfire.

The day was broiling hot and the schoolchildren had been sent home. The air was thick with orange smoke. Breathing was difficult. The acrid of smell of fear oozing from people's pores. The winds were gusting over one hundred kilometres per hour and the fires were merging into a fast moving firestorm. The afternoon temperate hit thirty-eight degrees. Strickland Avenue was burning and the Browns River fire swept up over Sleeping Beauty and joined the Mount Wellington fire, spreading into Fern Tree. The hotel, shop and parish hall were burning, as were many of the houses. Fallen trees blocked the roads, and people were piling into cars with cats, dogs and chickens. Her parents tried to push her into a car with strangers who were heading down Summerleas Road but she slipped from their grip and ran towards her home. With a whoosh and a crackle, the grass caught fire and the hot, smarting flames began licking her legs. For a moment, she couldn't tell hot from cold but, whatever it was, it stung like a jellyfish. As her home burst into flames, shattering all the windows, someone swept her into their arms, pulled off her melting shoes and socks and rushed her away.

The man's grey gimlet eyes glazed over. His presence cast a pall, silencing every living thing on the mountain. She stood mute.

The man returned week after week, watching over her shoulder as she worked, drinking tea, telling her stories of his life, making notes in a little book he kept in his top pocket and, despite his lack, she took comfort in companionship.

Then one day, apropos of nothing, he turned and touched her hair and asked her why she never coloured it blonde. She put down her pen, threw open the French doors, strode into her garden and crouched down beside her vegetable patch. Her scars tightened and recalled the exquisite pain of the debridement. Her legs, the topography of the land. Picking up a trowel, she began to turn the soil to free the kale and silverbeet seedlings from encroaching weeds. The soil was chocolate brown and brimming with life.

The man followed, casting a long shadow. As though an advertisement for an advertisement, he told her that she could do anything these days, even get blue contact lenses to change the brown of her eyes.

Jamming the trowel in the soil, her body flashed with the heat of rage and she stood and asked him to leave.

Currawongs were busy pulling loose nails from the roof and dropping them, watching them roll into the gutter, clanging and chiming as they went. They started as his car door slammed and they watched him sitting in the cabin for ten minutes or more as if waiting for her to change her mind.

The last of the snows had melted, filling the rivers and streams with clear, cold water. She began walking to the springs, filling bottles and packing them in her backpack. Walking cleansed her mind, spring water cooled the rage and she resumed a solitary life. Loneliness clawing her from the inside out.

Some weeks later, the man returned, turned the door handle and tiptoed inside.

The ruckus they made was plain. A warning so loud, thirty or more currawongs came down from the mountain to see what the fuss was all about, hopeful of a feed. They too sensed imminent danger and lined up along the wires of the hills hoist, joining me in a loud chorus of 'kar-wheek-wheek-kar' but she took no notice. One flew down to the windowsill and pecked at the glass but it was too late.

The woman was finishing a cushion plant drawing, head down. Focused. Pulling a wire from his pocket, the man held a wooden toggle in each hand and in one fast movement whipped it over her head and pulled it tight around her neck. Her legs and arms flailed and thrashed, knocking her inkpot over her drawing. Pens and pencils toppled over and rolled off the desk and the only the sound left was a killer's shallow, rapid breath.

Lifting her body off the chair, he lay her on the floor and went outside to her garden shed. He took a shovel and dug a hole at the edge of the garden then dragged her across the lawn and rolled her into her shallow grave. He stamped down the mound and covered it with leaf-litter. He washed brown dirt from his hands and wiped them dry on his trousers. Hurrying inside, he took several details of her work, nodded to himself and left.

The woman had no kin and no friends. Nobody came. Nobody noticed.

Spring passed into summer. Young birds demanded food and learned to fly. The wind blew hot from the north.

Currawongs scratched at the earth until the tip of the woman's finger emerged from the shallow grave. 'Kar-week-week-kar' they called and pecked at it until it came loose. There was a brief squabble for the prize until one bird picked it up in my beak and flew to the nearest house and dropped it in the middle of the doormat.

Blue and red flashing lights cast their carnival colours along the gum trunks. Police officers questioned the neighbours, who pointed to the woman's cottage. They dusted her house for fingerprints, searched her drawings and scanned her notebooks. It wasn't long before the man was identified, charged and in custody.

Forensics exhumed the woman's body, wrapped her remains in a plastic, and placed them on a sling and into the back of a van.

As they drove away, a flock of currawongs formed a guard of honour along the wires of her Hills hoist and the mountain wind howled a requiem.

A diminutive woman with a fertile imagination perched on the edge of a stool at her desk, her feet evenly placed along the foot rail, her gold-rimmed glasses pushed up into her hair as she drew a rare dainty leek orchid. Alone.

There had been a fire, a man an insult. He had taken details of her work and submitted them as his own as if he had stolen her very breath.

Solitude returned and settled in like an old friend and,, once again, she was as an atoll in a roiling sea. The bridges and ports closed. The lighthouse lamp extinguished.